. . . for parents and teachers

The average television set is on for seven hours a day. By age six, children have spent more time receiving TV's programmed messages than they will spend during their first eight years in a school classroom.

What is learned through that passive absorption of an electron beam? What isn't learned? We're not sure — and that's the scariest part of it. Do children, for example, forget how to imagine their own adventures? Do they remember what to do with a sunny day and an open field? *The Day Our TV Broke Down* deals with these very questions.

This is an important story. It dares to suggest that Saturdays can still be good days — even when TV cartoons are missing. And real people in the real world can be even more interesting than *Super Mouse* and *Wonder Cat*. Children must be reminded that there is more magic inside themselves than inside the TV set.

But first, as this story demonstrates, adults need to remind *themselves* of the magic in the real world.

THOMAS L. HOLBROOK, M.D.
MEDICAL DIRECTOR, ROGERS
HOSPICE
ROGERS MEMORIAL HOSPITAL
OCONOMOWOC, WISCONSIN

Betty Ren Wright is the author of nearly forty books for children. She lives in Wisconsin.

Library of Congress Number: 80-14434

1 2 3 4 5 6 7 8 9 0 84 83 82 81 80

Printed in the United States of America.

Library of Congress Cataloging in Publication Data

Wright, Betty Ren.
    The day our TV broke down.

    SUMMARY: When the television breaks down, a cartoon addict discovers he enjoys other activities also.
    [1. Television — Fiction] I. Bejna, Barbara.
II. Jensen, Shirlee. III. Title.
PZ7.W933Day   [Fic]   80-14434
ISBN 0-8172-1365-1

THE DAY
OUR TV
BROKE DOWN

by *Betty Ren Wright*

illustrated by Barbara Bejna and Shirlee Jensen

introduction by Thomas L. Holbrook, M.D.

RAINTREE CHILDRENS BOOKS

Milwaukee • Toronto • Melbourne • London

Saturday is D-Day. D for Dad.

Every Saturday my Dad picks me up and
takes me to breakfast at a restaurant. Then
we go to his apartment, and I stay there
all day.

Mostly I watch cartoons on TV.
Saturday is the best day for doing that.

Sometimes, Dad says, "Let's go out and have fun."

Or he says, "Let's talk for a while."

Or he gets a little bit angry and says, "You watch TV too much."

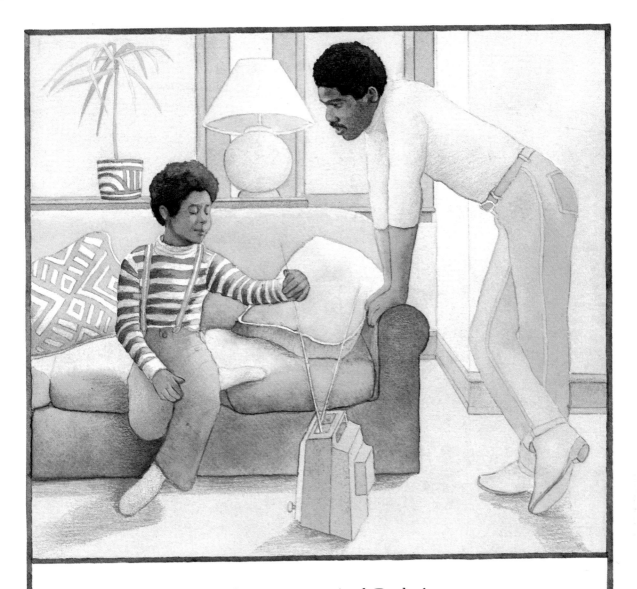

But I *like* cartoons. And Dad always
keeps busy. He reads or washes his socks
while I watch TV.

At noon we go to a drive-in for lunch.
That's always fun.

After lunch Dad always has to watch the games on TV. He watches football, baseball, and soccer. I watch with him, or I look at magazines, or I work on puzzles. Sometimes I get bored.

I say, "Let's go out and have fun."

I say, "Let's talk."

Or I try to sound angry and say, "You watch TV too much."

Dad just laughs.

Then, when the games are over, Dad takes me home. "See you next Saturday," he says, and he gives me a hug.

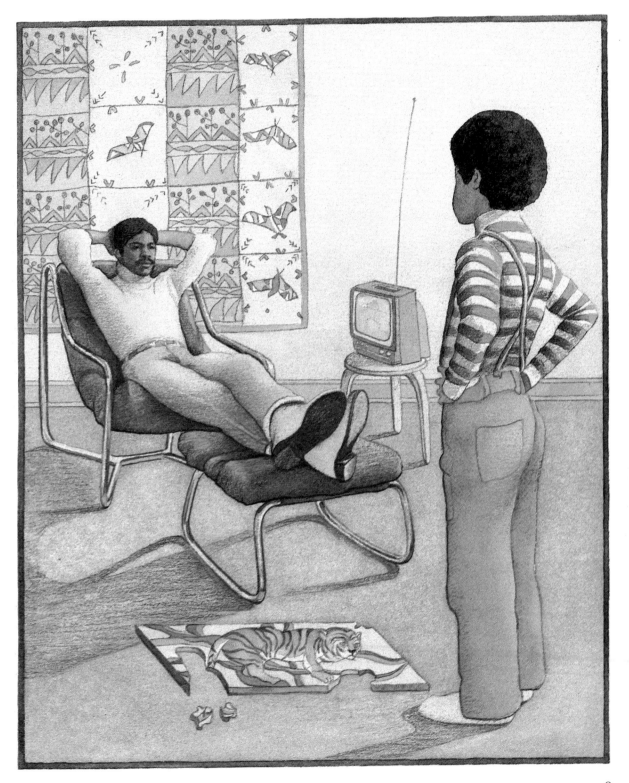

9

Last Saturday we went to a new restaurant for breakfast. I had chocolate doughnuts. I just knew it was going to be a good day.

We went to Dad's apartment. It was time for *Super Mouse*. I flipped on the TV.

"You watch TV too much —" Dad started to say.

Just then, the TV screen went black. *Super Mouse* was gone.

"Oh, no!" I yelled.

Dad turned the knobs. We could hear *Super Mouse*, but we couldn't see him. I felt like crying.

"I'll call the repair shop," Dad said.

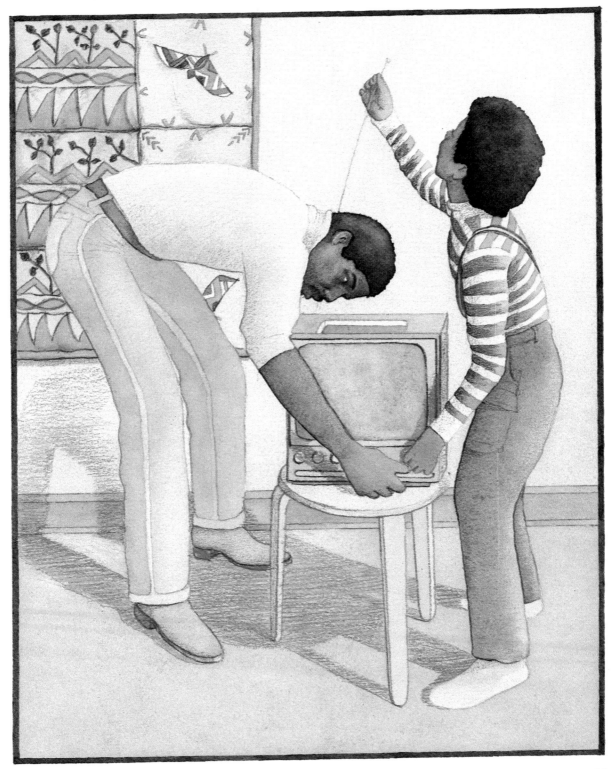

I walked around the apartment. There was nothing to do. Nothing at all.

"Tell the repairman to hurry," I shouted.

But I knew it was no use. *Super Mouse* was almost over by that time. *Wonder Cat* would start soon. Even if a repairman came in two minutes, I would miss both shows.

Dad came back from the phone. "Well," he said, "what shall we do now?"

"Nothing," I mumbled.

"Come on — think," he said. "There are other ways of having fun."

I couldn't think of a single thing.

"I guess we could make cookies," I said finally. "Do you have a mix?"

He didn't.

"I'll go to the store," I said. I tried to
sound as though I were having lots of fun,
but I was still thinking about *Wonder Cat*.

It was a sunny day. There was a field
next to Dad's apartment building. A girl
my size was practicing soccer.

"Hey, do you want to play?" she
shouted at me.

"No, thanks," I said. "I have to
make cookies."

At the corner, I stopped to watch
some machines.

"Watch that shovel," a man told me.
"It's digging a basement for a new
apartment building."

I watched. The shovel had dragon teeth
and a dragon roar. It took big bites out of
the ground. The basement got deeper.
I almost forgot about the cookies.

I remembered the cookies, but just
before I got to the store, I saw the library.
I decided to stop in and check out a few
books. I didn't know how long it was
going to be before the TV was fixed.

It took me a long time to find just the
right books. . . .

When I finally got back, Dad was waiting. "Just because my TV broke down is no reason to leave forever," he teased.

"Sorry," I said. "Are you hungry for cookies?"

"I'm starved," he said. "But I'm afraid we won't be able to go out for lunch for a while. We have to be here when the TV repairman comes."

"We'll have lunch here," I said. "We know what's for dessert — cookies. I'll make peanut butter sandwiches. You make cocoa."

We had fun making lunch together. While we waited for the cookies to finish baking, we looked at one of my library books.

"This was one of the best lunches I ever had," Dad said. "But I wonder where that repairman is. There's a really big game I wanted to watch this afternoon."

"You know, there are other ways of having fun besides TV," I said, trying to sound like Dad.

He didn't laugh. He just walked back
and forth. He looked out the window.
I felt sorry for him.

"Let's go out and play ball," I said.
"We can watch for the repairman while
we play."

The field was empty. Dad and I made
up a new kind of soccer game for just
two players.

Once I got to tackle Dad. "This is great!" I laughed. "I like this ball game much better than the ones on TV!"

25

Then I said, "Want to see a dragon?"
Dad looked confused, until we got to
the corner. There was the dragon, still
gobbling up the earth. An ice-cream truck
was there too.

On the way back to the apartment, we
met a puppy. It was white with long ears.

"He belongs to Mrs. Ferraro in my
building," Dad said. "We'd better take
him home."

Just then, the TV repair truck pulled up
in front of the building.

"I'll take him," I said. "You go help the
TV man."

The puppy was warm and wiggly. He
seemed glad I was helping him. Mrs.
Ferraro was glad too.

"You must come to visit Beenie
someday," she said.

When I got back to Dad's apartment,
the TV was working again.

"I'm sorry you missed the cartoons,"
Dad said.

"Well, I'm not," I said. "Dad, this was
the best Saturday I can remember."

"You really think so?" he asked. "You
know, I think you're right."

"And next Saturday," I said, "I'm going
to play ball with the girl next door. And
you and I will visit the dragon. And we'll
take Beenie for a walk. We'll make fudge
and read a book together. Then, if there's
time, I might watch *Wonder Cat*.

"It will be another great day," I said.